# Werewolf, Come Home

**More Devilish Fun with C.D. Bitesky, Howie Wolfner, Elisa and Frankie Stein, and Danny Keegan**
*From Avon Camelot*

### THE FIFTH GRADE MONSTERS SERIES

# Werewolf, Come Home

## Mel Gilden

Illustrated by John Pierard

A GLC BOOK

AN AVON  CAMELOT BOOK

WEREWOLF, COME HOME is an original publication of Avon Books. This work has never before appeared in book form.

AVON BOOKS
A division of
The Hearst Corporation
105 Madison Avenue
New York, New York 10016

Text and illustrations copyright © 1990 by General Licensing Company, Inc.
Published by arrangement with General Licensing Company, Inc.
Developed by Byron Preiss and Dan Weiss
Library of Congress Catalog Card Number: 90-93154
ISBN: 0-380-75908-X
RL: 4.4

First Avon Camelot Printing: October 1990

CAMELOT TRADEMARK REG. U.S. PAT. OFF. AND IN OTHER COUNTRIES. MARCA REGISTRADA. HECHO EN U.S.A.

Printed in the U.S.A.

OPM   10  9  8  7  6  5  4  3  2  1

# Chapter One

# The Familiaides Arrive

When his dog howled and tried to stuff himself under the living room couch, Danny Keegan knew that Howie Wolfner was near. Danny stuck his place marker into *The Wonderful Flight to the Mushroom Planet*, flung the book onto the couch, and began to tug on his dog.

On a big deck of cardboard in the middle of the floor, his sister, Barbara, and his father were building a fort out of ice cream sticks. Barbara was trying to earn yet another Girls' Pathfinders merit badge. Angrily, she said, "What's the matter with Harryhausen?"

"Yes," said Mr. Keegan. "Can't that dog see we're doing delicate work here?" He carefully set a stick on top of a wall of them and scrunched up his face to study what he had done.

"I'll take him outside," Danny said. "You let Howie in." He pulled Harryhausen from under the couch and held him like a baby. Harryhausen wriggled and licked Danny's face but never both at once.

"How do you know Howie's here?" Mr. Keegan said.

That was a tough one, and Danny realized he'd made a mistake. The reason Danny knew about Howie was the way Harryhausen had just frantically tried to bury himself under the couch. Harryhausen acted that way because Howie was a werewolf, and like all animals, Harryhausen had a morbid fear of werewolves. Howie was the only werewolf the Keegan family was expecting that afternoon.

Danny said, "Howie said he'd be here about four on Sunday afternoon. Isn't it almost that now?"

Danny sighed when his father nodded. Barbara knew that Howie was one of Danny's monster friends, but his parents, like most of the adults in Danny's life, would have been very surprised to hear that Howie was a werewolf. Whether they would believe it or not was another question.

Danny carried Harryhausen through the kitchen where his mom was applying a screwdriver to the handle of the refrigerator door. As she turned the screwdriver a rattling stopped.

"Loose again?" Danny said.

"Yes. Where are you going with Harryhausen?"

The door bell rang and Danny said, "Howie's here."

"How do you know?"

This time, Danny had an answer ready. He said, "Somebody's at the door. I hope it's Howie. Don't you?"

"It would be an improvement over somebody trying to sell us something we don't need."

Danny agreed and went out the back door. The air

2

was warm and heavy with the fragrance of flowers in Mrs. Keegan's garden. Harryhausen wouldn't freeze or anything. Danny filled his dish with fresh water and hooked a long chain to Harryhausen's collar. Harryhausen would be able to roam the entire backyard without actually being able to leave it.

Danny scratched Harryhausen behind the ears and ran inside the house where he found his family talking to Howie. A fat blue suitcase stood on the floor next to him. He was carrying his skateboard.

"Hey, Howie!"

"What ho, Danny! How are you, old chum?" Howie had a British accent. To Danny, he sounded like a guy in a spy movie. At first glance, Howie looked like an ordinary fifth grade boy—though a little cleaner than most. It was only later that anyone noticed Howie's reddish brown hair grew a little low on the forehead, that his teeth were a little too sharp, that his ears were a little too pointed, and that the black smudge on his nose was not dirt.

"Great," said Danny. "How's Mount Palomine?"

"Simply capital. Out in the wilds of Connecticut there are no city lights to interfere with my parents' observations. Through the observatory telescope the moon looks bigger than a dinner plate, and the planetarium show is ripping."

"We're delighted to have you for the week," Mrs. Keegan said, "but we don't have to spend it here in the hallway. Danny, why don't you take Howie upstairs and help him get settled?"

Howie picked up his suitcase and said, "My parents are most grateful for your hospitality. They absolutely guarantee they will be here to pick me up early Friday evening."

"No problem," said Mr. Keegan.

"But you couldn't stay up in the mountains with them because you have to go to school," Barbara said as if it were a defect in Howie's character.

Howie laughed and said, "But I must go to school." He led Danny up the stairs, taking them two at a time.

Danny, Barbara, and Howie walked to school with Ryan Webler, the new kid on the block. He was chocolate brown and had a soft explosion of black hair. In one hand he carried a bag lunch and in the other a slim white suitcase that Danny knew contained a laptop computer.

Ryan said, "When your parents get back I'd like to talk to them about their astronomical discoveries. I'm going to write an article for the school paper." Howie knew his parents would be delighted.

At school, the hot topic was the special episode of *Mother Scary's Matinee*. Mother Scary was the host of a TV program that showed old monster movies. Normally, the program was on Saturday afternoons, but this week only it would be on Friday night. Mother Scary promised a special show, but only she and a few others knew exactly what it would be.

Mother Scary was the stage name of Zelda Bella, a woman the kids met back when she was selling fruit and Howie was trying to become a real boy. Since then, they'd found out she was actually a witch. Once, the wrong people found that out, and she needed the kids' help so she wouldn't be sent back to Rumania, where she'd been born.

At recess, while Danny and Ryan and the monster kids stood under their tree at one corner of the school yard, Frankie Stein explained fractions to them. Ryan wasn't listening. He was sitting beneath the tree typing. His laptop computer clicked and hummed.

Frankie was the tallest kid in the fifth grade; he was even taller than some of the kids in the sixth grade. He had stiff bristly hair that resisted combing, and he always carried colored pens in his shirt pocket. The strangest thing about him was that he had knobs on either side of his neck. His sister, Elisa, had them too. Her hair had a gray lightning streak up one side. When either of them spoke, their speech had a definite German accent.

Gilly Finn continued to shake her head, making her long blonde hair move in waves while she sang, " 'Bewitched, bothered, and bewildered, am I. . . .' " She had a big theatrical voice, and she liked to use it at dramatic moments. As a matter of fact, for her, all the world was a stage, and it seemed to Danny that she was always performing, even if he was the only other person in the room. Gilly was a slim girl who wore a short sea green dress and blue tights. Sometimes her hair looked a little green too. In the right light, Danny could almost see the wispy fins at her wrists and ankles.

C.D. Bitesky bowed and said, "You must believe in fractions, Gilly, before you can use them." He spoke in a lilting Transylvanian way that reminded Danny of old black and white horror movies. C.D. was the shortest kid in the fifth grade, but he was also the best dressed. He always wore a tuxedo and a black cape with a red satin lining. From a pocket in the cape he pulled a Thermos bottle and sucked red stuff from it through a straw he put between his tiny fangs. The red stuff was Fluid of Life, and it was all C.D. ever ate.

"Yo, knob head," called a piercing voice. A boy swaggered over to them.

"Hello, Stevie," Elisa said. She made an effort to be polite to Stevie Brickwald long after the other kids decided it was pointless.

"I hear you guys are building something for Mother Scary," Stevie said.

"That is true," Elisa said. "Gilly designed it, and Frankie and I are building it."

"That's what it says in the TV listings. But what it don't say is what the thing is."

Ryan looked up from his typing and said, "Nobody knows. The TV station isn't telling. They didn't even tell me and I'm writing an article about Mother Scary for the school paper."

"The station isn't telling, but knob head and fish face can tell."

"What charm you have," Howie said sarcastically.

Gilly said, "It'll be boffo, Stevie. Trust me."

"What is this 'boffo' garbage?"

"It's show biz talk for a big success."

"I don't care whether it's a success or not. I just want to know what it is."

"Somebody else talk to him," Gilly said as she turned away. "He's giving me a headache."

"Hey," said Stevie as he raised a fist and took a step in Gilly's direction. Frankie and Elisa closed up

**6**

in front of him like a pair of sliding doors, blocking his way. Frankie held up a finger and made lightning jump from it.

Stevie lowered his fist but did not open it. He said, "Yeah, this *whole thing* gives me a headache. Mother Scary gives me a headache. I probably won't even be home Friday night. I got things to do." He stalked off.

Ryan said, "I don't suppose you'd tell us. Your good friends. So I could put it in the article."

Elisa shook her head and said, "We promised."

"Hey, Gilly," Ryan called, "how do you spell 'boffo'?"

Every day after school Danny and Howie went to the Talbot Arms, the big modern apartment building where the Wolfners lived, to pick up the mail. Danny rode his bicycle and Howie slid along on his skateboard.

The building was made of sparkly white stone and was thirty stories high. Howie lived with his family at the very top, in the penthouse.

On Thursday, Danny did what he always did: He left his bicycle with the uniformed doorman and went with Howie to the main desk.

"Post for Wolfner?" Howie said.

"Oh, sure," the woman behind the desk said, "the mail." From below her desk she pulled a magazine, some envelopes, and a cardboard box big enough to hold a dozen doughnuts.

Howie went through the stack. "Bills. Bills. My parents' issue of *Moonglow*. More bills. Ah, this looks promising." He read the label on the cardboard box and exclaimed, "It's for me!"

7

"What is it?" Danny said.

"Come upstairs and I'll show you."

As they rode up in the elevator, Howie smiled to himself. He held the box next to his ear and shook it gently. Danny stared at the box, wishing he had X-ray vision, wondering what was inside. At the thirtieth floor Howie pushed the floor buttons in a particular order and the elevator doors slid open.

The Wolfner penthouse looked as if it were made of hand-rubbed wood. Needlepoint cushions padded the chairs and the lamps were made of a polished brass that seemed to shine with its own yellow light. Paintings on the walls showed big animals like deer being pulled down by packs of wolves or wild dogs. To Danny, it seemed to be a place where a lot of thinking was done.

Howie dumped the mail on the kitchen table where it joined the mail of previous days, and inspected the house. He walked through room after room, making sure that everything was the way his parents had left it. Danny heard Howie's hollow footsteps as he wandered around his mom's rooftop observatory. Howie climbed down the stairs and they went into his room, where they found a brown dog curled at the foot of the bed. It was mechanical dog, made of bronze and studded with thousands of rivets. Howie petted it but it did not move. "Should I turn Bruno on?" Howie said.

"You'll just have to turn him off again. You know what your parents said about leaving him on when nobody's around."

"Indeed," said Howie and shook his head.

"What's in the box?" Danny said.

Howie shook himself and said, "Right-o, the box." He led the way back through the living room, picking up an old copy of *Moonglow* along the way and thumbing through it. In the kitchen, he threw the box to Danny. It didn't weigh much, as if it might be filled with shredded wheat. The return address was Zenith Novelties, London, England.

"What's a Zenith Novelties?"

"That's just the company. Look here." Howie shoved the magazine at Danny. It was open to a page with a lot of advertising on it. The heading said FILLING ALL YOUR NATURAL AND SUPERNATURAL NEEDS. There must have been a hundred individual ads, each in its own box. One of the boxes had been outlined in red pen. Inside the box was a fuzzy black and white picture of something that could have been a tadpole with arms and legs.

"Familiaides?" Danny said.

"Look here," Howie said and pulled the magazine away from him. Howie read from the ad: " 'Just dip the familiaide packet into fresh water and familiaides will leap forth, ready to do your bidding. Need an extra hand to clean up the cottage? To mix your brew? To hold your place in a book of spells? Familiaides are for you!' Super, isn't it?"

"Super, sure," Danny said. "What are you going to do with them?"

"I'm going to give them to Zelda Bella."

"Makes sense," Danny said and nodded.

"What's wrong, Danny? Where is your enthusiasm?"

"These familiaides will be great if they do what the ad says they'll do. But my experience with mail order stuff is that you don't always get what you expect. Maybe we should take a look.''

"I was hoping to allow Zelda Bella the honor of opening the cardboard box.''

Danny was not convinced it would be an honor, but he said, "I think there's time to visit Zelda Bella at Halloween Acres before we have to be home.'' He really wanted to see what was inside that box. Familiaides?

# Chapter Two

# Witching to Be Done

It was a long ride to Halloween Acres, out near where Long Island started to get wild, but there was still plenty of light when Danny and Howie got off the bus.

Halloween Acres was a retirement community. Some of the old people who lived there were ordinary, but most of them were witches or warlocks. A lot of individual houses were sprinkled over the rolling parkland and connected by stone paths. Here and there cauldrons hung over barbeque pits. Cats were everywhere, and not all of them were black. They pretty much stayed away from Howie.

They hadn't been to Halloween Acres for a while, so Danny and Howie had to study the big posted map before they could find Zelda Bella's condo. After they walked there and Danny knocked on the door, a peephole opened and a wild eye looked out at them. The person behind the door cried, "Well, as I live and breathe," and swung the door open. "What a nice surprise, boys, visiting a lonely old woman like this. Come in. Come in.''

Zelda Bella was almost as wide as she was tall. She wore what Danny thought of as Gypsy clothes. Neither her dress nor her blouse was made of a single piece of cloth, but of many pieces of cloth sewn together, each one seemingly chosen to clash with all the others. Loud plaids butted up against star patterns and stuff that looked like optical illusions. If C.D.'s father, who was a tailor, had been there, he might have been able to sort it all out.

The living room was just as Danny remembered it. The furniture was old and heavy and most pieces had legs carved into the feet of animals. Every horizontal surface had a little statue or something on it. The big grandfather clock clicked off what remained of eternity. The room had a lot of Zelda Bella's personality.

"Are you lonely, Zelda Bella?' Howie said.

Zelda Bella blushed and waved at them once as she fell back onto her couch. "Are you kidding? My fans won't leave me alone. Hollywood is calling with offers. What would you think of *Mother Scary: the Motion Picture*?''

"Wow,'' Howie and Danny said together.

"We're just talking so far. To what do I owe this visit? Trying to be a real boy again, Howie? More evil folks trying to send all the monsters back where they came from?''

"Actually,'' said Howie, "we brought you a gift.'' He handed the cardboard box to Zelda Bella. "To help with the special show tomorrow night.''

"What's a Zenith Novelties?'' Zelda Bella said.

Danny said, "That's just the company. Go ahead and open it."

Zelda Bella rolled to her feet and toddled into the kitchen. The boys followed. In the center of the room was a big cauldron filled with water. "I was just about to make some Shakespeare soup," Zelda Bella said as she pawed through drawers.

"Shakespeare soup?" Howie said.

Zelda Bella turned around with a pair of scissors in her hand. She conducted herself as she spoke. "You know, like in Shakespeare's play, *Macbeth*:

> " *'Fillet of a fenny snake,*
> *In the cauldron boil and bake;*
> *Eye of newt and toe of frog,*
> *Wool of bat and tongue of dog . . .'* "

"Tongue of dog?" Howie asked uncomfortably.

Danny wondered how C.D. would feel about "wool of bat."

Zelda Bella lowered her scissors and said, "Actually, that's just poetry. The soup I had in mind is really vegetable." She pointed the scissors at the sink where carrots and celery and other vegetables were lined up.

Howie sighed and said, "Open the box."

"Right. Right." Zelda Bella set the box on the kitchen table and like a surgeon carefully cut it open. Inside the box was a sheet of printed instructions wrapped around a cellophane bag containing what looked like short lengths of dry brown rope. Zelda Bella held the bag in one hand and the instructions in the other. "Familiaides?" she said.

"Instant help. Just add water," Howie said, and laughed.

"That's what it says." Zelda Bella shook her head and chuckled. "You know, I've seen ads for familiaides in the back of *Broom and Cauldron* magazine for years but it never occurred to me to actually send away for them." She hefted the bag and said, "Should we do it, boys?"

Suddenly, Danny wasn't so sure; strange things sometimes arrived in the mail. But he said, "Go ahead. I'm dying of curiosity."

Howie nodded. "Me too."

"Sure," said Zelda Bella. "I can make soup anytime." She mumbled as she read the instructions. "Seems simple enough," she said. She put down the paper and dropped the bag into the cauldron. Seconds later the water began to churn with activity. Danny could see black things swimming in it.

All three of them fell back when something leaped from the cauldron and stood on the narrow edge looking around and flexing its arms and legs. It was black and the size of a frog. It looked like a Pacman creature or a happy face with thin arms and legs. The face had round eyes like gummed looseleaf reinforcements and a thin slash of a smile.

More familiaides leaped from the water and began to do impossible exercises there on the edge of the cauldron. It looked to Danny like a familiaide aerobics class.

The familiaides noticed Zelda Bella and the boys, and with tiny screams of delight leaped at them. Danny held up his arms to ward them off, but the familiaides turned out to be no more vicious than kittens. They climbed all over him, tickling as they went and making small contented noises, but they didn't hurt at all. They felt as if they were made of leather even softer than his dad's bomber jacket.

"Friendly little guys," Zelda Bella said.

"Jolly right you are."

"All right, men," Zelda Bella said in a voice of command. "Enough of this lollygagging around. Line up." She drew an imaginary line on the kitchen floor with a toe.

The familiaides jumped to the floor and lined up at attention. Danny was impressed. Zelda Bella walked up and back in front of them with her hands behind her back. "Men," she said, "I have a special show to do tomorrow night and you can help me with it. Tricks need to be prepared, jokes need to be written, spells need to be looked up."

The familiaides nodded.

"Right then, men. To the basement. There's witching to be done." She pointed to the doorway and marched—arms swinging, knees high—out of the kitchen. The line of familiaides followed her, even imitating the way she marched.

Danny and Howie marched along after until Zelda Bella poked her head back into the kitchen. "Thanks for the familiaides, Howie. They'll come in real handy. Can you guys find your own way out?"

"Of course," Howie said.

Zelda Bella went away. She shouted, "Onward, men!"

"I guess that was a success," Danny said.

"Blimy if it wasn't."

As they let themselves out Zelda Bella's front door, Danny could hear crashing and banging in the basement. He wondered again if the familiaides were all they seemed to be.

# Chapter Three

# Howie Needs a Haircut

Howie rode his skateboard to school on Friday, so he got there before Danny and Barbara. When Danny joined his monster friends, Gilly and the Stein kids were huddled together by themselves.

"Large doings," C.D. said. He sucked on his Fluid of Life while he watched Elisa and Frankie and Gilly.

"Indeed," said Howie. "Those three have been thick as thieves. And they refuse to discuss their part in Mother Scary's special show." He rubbed his forehead.

"Did you tell them about the familiaides?" Danny said.

"Of course," Howie said. "Frankie said they wouldn't be necessary, but Gilly thought she could train them to dance in a chorus line like the Rockettes."

"Familiaides?" Ryan said. "Am I the only one here without a secret?"

"You are not," C.D. said. He looked meaningfully at Howie and Danny. They explained about the familiaides.

When they were done, C.D. said, "In the old country I have heard of familiars. They are small animals that help witches and warlocks. A familiaide is like that?"

"Better than that," Howie said. "Modern, new, more convenient because they're freeze-dried and guaranteed."

"Radical," said Ryan. "I'll want a consumer report for the school paper."

"Capital, old chum. I'm certain Zelda Bella will be easy to interview."

"Yeah," said Danny. "Ask her one question and stand back."

Howie rubbed his forehead again and said, "Warm today, isn't it?"

"About normal for this time of year," Ryan said. Howie shook his head.

"What is the matter?" C.D. said.

"I don't know." He vigorously scratched his forehead where a point of hair came down and nearly touched the bridge of his nose. "I'm hot and itchy."

Ryan and Danny backed off and Danny said, "I hope you don't have the flu."

"No flu I've ever had felt like this."

"You have more hair than normal," C.D. said.

"Maybe I need a haircut. I don't know."

The bell rang and everybody went inside. Howie rolled up his shirt sleeves and continued to scratch his forehead. Danny wondered when he himself would start to feel hot and itchy. After all, he and Howie had been living in the same house all week. On the other hand, maybe Danny wouldn't get it at all because whatever Howie had was some werewolf thing. That possibility relieved Danny some, but he was still worried about Howie.

During social studies, Ms. Cosgrove had to ask Howie a question three times before he even responded, and then he asked to have the question repeated. Generally, Howie was one of the first to raise a hand.

"Are you feeling OK, Howie?" Ms. Cosgrove said.

"He's OK, Ms. Cosgrove. He always looks like that," Stevie Brickwald said and snorted a laugh.

"Please, Stevie."

"I'm fine," Howie said sleepily. He scratched his forehead absent-mindedly. Danny was certain that Howie's hair had grown since that morning—grown a lot more than normal, even for Howie. He was positively shaggy.

"I think you'd better go to the nurse."

"Jolly good," Howie said, but instead of standing up, he rested his head on his arms.

Ms. Cosgrove asked Frankie to walk Howie to the nurse's office. Danny supposed, it was just in case Howie fell over and somebody had to carry him. Frankie was the only one in class who could do it.

The lesson went on without Howie, but Danny and his monster friends traded a lot of meaningful looks. What was wrong with Howie?

At recess, instead of going outside, Danny and his friends went to the nurse's office to visit him. The nurse, Miss Cubbage, was sitting at her desk filling in forms. She was a thin woman who wore big round glasses and always sat or stood very straight. She

19

wore practical shoes, rounded clunky things that looked like the shoes of a cartoon character. When she saw the crowd that had come to visit she said, "Two of you may go in. The rest of you wait in the hall. We can't be overexciting our patient."

Danny didn't know why seeing his friends would overexcite Howie, but he and the other kids went out into the hall to talk things over.

Elisa said, "Danny should go. He is Howie's host."

Danny shrugged and smiled. He wanted to see Howie, but he didn't want to catch whatever Howie had. He forced himself not to worry about it and said, "Miss Cubbage said Howie could have two visitors."

"Maybe I should go," Ryan said. "As a reporter, I can *get the story*."

C.D. shook his head. "I am sorry not to agree. I must go because Howie's background and mine are similar. One might call me a werebat. Perhaps I can be of assistance where someone else might not."

"C.D.'s right," Gilly said. "It'll take more than a smile and a shoe shine to help Howie."

The kids agreed that Danny and C.D. were the two to make the visit.

"I'll expect a full report," Ryan said.

Elisa said, "We all will."

Howie and C.D. went back into the nurse's office and Miss Cubbage smiled them into the next room.

When he saw Howie, Danny was astonished and a little horrified. He could tell by the look on C.D.'s face, and by the speed with which he was sucking up Fluid of Life, that he felt the same. They'd both seen Howie in wolf form, but the condition had always been temporary, and there had always been a reason for it. This time, Howie seemed to be changing for no reason at all.

Howie was sitting cross-legged in the middle of a cot, digging at his socks with hands that had shrunk into things very like paws. He was even hairier than he had been before. His nose was longer and blacker, and his ears came to definite points. Danny wondered when Miss Cubbage had last looked in on her patient. When Howie saw Danny and C.D. he began to pant.

Danny said, "How are you doing, Howie?"

What Howie said may have been the word "fine," but it sounded more like the yelp of an unhappy dog.

"Maybe there's garlic around here somewhere," Danny said. "That always makes him turn into a wolf."

C.D. shook his head. "There is no garlic. Trust me."

Danny remembered that garlic always turned C.D. into a bat. "Well, then it's something else. He was in my house. Howie, is there something at my house that did this to you?"

Howie didn't say anything. He just lifted one foot and used it to scratch under his chin.

Danny was impressed. "We have to do something," he said as he watched Howie with morbid fascination. "He's turning into a wolf for no reason."

"There is always a reason."

"Yes. But what?"

"I do not know. I am unable to assist Howie, after all. Maybe one of the others will have an idea."

Howie pulled a blanket around himself with his long sharp teeth, and shut his eyes.

"Sleep will be good for him," C.D. said.

"Maybe he'll wake up a boy again as he usually does."

"Perhaps. But I do not think we can depend on this."

Danny nodded. "Anyway, with the blanket over him like that, Miss Cubbage won't notice how much he looks like a wolf."

"Maybe. We can hope."

They came out of the back room and thanked Miss Cubbage for allowing them to visit. "He'll be fine," she said and smiled at them. She shook her head. "Even if he *does* need a haircut."

Out in the hall, Danny and C.D. made their report. When they finished, Gilly said, "Whew! We got trouble. Right here at P.S. 13." She shook her head and no one said anything. The kids all seemed to be thinking. Danny suddenly became aware that they were inside the school building during recess. Such a thing was almost unknown. It was quiet and he could feel how empty the building was.

"We have to liberate him," Ryan said.

"Liberate?" Frankie said.

"We have to take him someplace where he'll be safe, and we have to do it now, before Miss Cubbage sees him. Otherwise the jig will be up."

"Jig?" C.D. said. "You must learn to speak English."

Ryan shot C.D. a look of amazement.

"Ryan means the fact that Howie is a werewolf will be all over school," Gilly said. "Then it'll be all over town."

The kids were nodding, and Danny was trying to think of a plan when Miss Cubbage screamed.

"We are too late," C.D. said.

As they ran back into the nurse's office Howie howled in a way that raised the hackles on the back of Danny's neck. He could imagine the paint on the walls peeling. Howie ran past them and out into the hall, looking more like a big wolf than Danny had ever seen him. He and the others ran after him, but a four-footed Howie was very fast, and when they got to the corner of the hallway, he was gone. Far away they heard him howl again. They ran back to the nurse's office.

Miss Cubbage was sprawled on the floor looking confused. As Frankie and Ryan helped her to the cot, Elisa said, "What happened?"

Miss Cubbage touched one hand to her chest and said, "I don't quite know."

Gilly offered her a glass of water. Miss Cubbage took it and drank a few sips.

"How'd you do that?" Danny whispered, thinking that she'd sung the water up. Gilly was very good with water.

"I got it from the tap," Gilly said. She pointed to a small bathroom where a paper cup dispenser hung next to the sink.

Danny didn't say anything, but he was a little surprised. He had to remind himself that, like his other friends, Gilly was a kid as well as a monster. She was bound to do something in a normal kid way sometimes.

Miss Cubbage lowered the paper cup and said, "I went to see how your friend was doing when this beast leaped at me."

"Beast?" C.D. said.

23

"Yes. Like a big dog or a wolf. It must have eaten your friend!" She sounded hysterical. Gilly gave her another cup of water. Miss Cubbage now had one in each hand. She looked from one to the other and took a sip.

"There is no evidence Howie was eaten," Frankie said.

Miss Cubbage looked around. The cot and the floor around it were clean. "No. Then what happened?"

"It's a mystery, all right," Gilly said.

"We'll have to find him. We can't have patients disappearing," Miss Cubbage said.

The kids agreed and the bell rang. "I'll be all right," Miss Cubbage said. "You children had better go back to class."

"What are you going to do?" Ryan said.

"I suppose I'll start by talking to Ms. Gunderson, the principal. Maybe she'll have an idea. You kids go to class."

Outside the office, the hallway was filling with the rumble of kids going back to their classrooms. "I'll be fine," Miss Cubbage said as if she were trying to convince herself as much as them.

Danny and the others straggled into the hall and walked toward Ms. Cosgrove's classroom, a small knot of worry. They had difficulty concentrating on their arithmetic lesson, and Danny's spelling test was a real disaster. From the groans he heard around him, he could tell he was not alone.

Occasionally, they heard Howie's howl and the class stopped. Even Ms. Cosgrove looked up. Each time, it took a few minutes for her to get back into the swing of teaching. Mr. Page, the custodian, ran by carrying a big butterfly net over his shoulder. He ran first one way, and then a few minutes later ran the other.

At lunch Danny and his friends kept a sharp eye out for Howie. But they neither saw nor heard him. Evidently he was hiding somewhere. Either that or he'd left P.S. 13. In which case, "the jig" as Ryan suggested, "was up."

"Sure," said Danny. "He looks like a wolf right now, which is OK, I guess. But what if he turns into a boy in front of somebody?"

Frankie said, "What if he doesn't turn into a boy at all?"

That gave them all something to think about.

Gilly said, "I wouldn't normally suggest this, but I think we have to cut school and look for Howie."

"What will we do if and when we find him?" Frankie said.

"I don't know."

"Howie can take care of himself," C.D. said.

"I've never cut school in my life," Danny said. The very thought made him queasy.

They continued to talk about finding Howie, but it was clear to Danny that the others were as uncomfortable with the idea of cutting school as he was. It would never happen.

While they talked, a really interesting rumor went around. It replaced Mother Scary's show as the hot topic of conversation. Arthur Finster ran up to Danny and his friends and said excitedly, "Have you heard? Miss. Cubbage was attacked by a wild animal!"

"When?" Danny said.

"During morning recess!"

"Is that so?" Ryan said. Danny knew it wasn't so. Like Ryan and the others, he'd been with Miss Cubbage during morning recess.

"Yeah!" said Arthur Finster and ran off to spread the word.

"Any minute now," said Gilly, "that wild beast will become a bear or something."

Gilly was nearly right. By the end of recess, the rumor came around again. This time it was that Miss Cubbage and Ms. Gunderson had both been barbecued by the breath of Godzilla. It didn't occur to anybody that if Godzilla were around, someone would very likely have seen him.

"Very creative," Elisa said.

"What about Howie?" C.D. said.

"School will last only another few hours," Elisa said. "He will be safe till then."

Danny hoped Elisa was right.

Time passed slowly. Oceans evaporated. The wind wore mountains down by entire inches. The only high spots during the afternoon were when the kids still sometimes heard Howie howling. The sound was encouraging because it didn't seem to be getting any farther away.

Just before three, when they were gathering their books and papers together and shutting down for the week, a howl sounded just outside the door of Ms. Cosgrove's room. Claws clattered on linoleum and a second later a hairy beast ran into the room. Kids shrieked and scattered. Ms. Cosgrove leaped onto her desk. Danny almost called out, "Howie!" but restrained himself. Howie ran into the cloakroom.

27

Mr. Page stood in the doorway, his butterfly net at the ready. He was a heroic figure in work shirt and jeans. He took the measure of the situation and said, "All right. Where is he?" Ms. Cosgrove pointed.

Mr. Page stalked his prey. But he had not gone three steps when something roared out of the cloak-room. It was Howie on his skateboard! He rolled around Mr. Page like four feet of thunder. Mr. Page took a swipe at him with his butterfly net but missed completely, catching the world globe instead. He mumbled, "Sorry" and ran after Howie.

It was unusually quiet in the room. Still atop her desk, Ms. Cosgrove said, "I guess there really is a beast."

The kids all began to talk at once. Many of them were disappointed that the beast was so small. They had been expecting Godzilla.

The bell rang but nobody was sure what to do. Danny guessed that they were worried about meeting the beast in the hall or on the way home.

Ms. Cosgrove laughed and climbed down from her desk. She said, "I guess we could all use a weekend about now. Class dismissed."

For a moment, nobody moved. "Go on," Ms. Cosgrove said with mock impatience. "Get out of here. Go home."

Kids started to straggle out. Most of them stood in the doorway and looked both ways before they ventured into the hallway. Nobody complained. Nobody pushed.

Danny and Ryan and the monster kids gathered outside the door. Elisa said, "Frankie and I cannot

28

help you hunt. We must finish the project we promised to Mother Scary.''

"We'll be OK," Gilly said. She did a little dance step and sang, " 'I have the cool, clear eyes of a seeker of wisdom and truth.' "

After Elisa and Frankie had gone, Danny said, "I really feel as if this is all my fault.''

"That is not certain," C.D. said.

"Yeah," said Danny, "but somebody has to take the blame and it might as well be me." He looked at Gilly, Ryan, and C.D. "Are you guys with me?''

"Like barnacles," Gilly said.

Ryan nodded. C.D. just bowed.

# Chapter Four

# Two Doctors, No Use

Danny found a pay phone in a Shop-Along-Cassidy convenience store near P.S. 13. He called and asked his mother if it would be OK for him and Howie to be a little late getting home from school; they'd be playing with Gilly and Ryan and C.D. The whole story was just about true. Mrs. Keegan said it was all right and promised to call Gilly's parents and Ryan's and C.D.'s.

"Now what?" said Danny as he stepped from under the phone's hood. As if in answer, they heard a howl that could only have been Howie's. And it wasn't far away.

"That way," Ryan cried and ran off. Danny and the others ran after him. Howie was in front of the school sniffing a bush. His skateboard was nowhere in sight. When he saw Danny and the others he yipped at them a time or two. His tail was wagging.

"Come on, Howie," said Gilly and approached him with her hand out. Howie danced away.

"Come on, Howie," said Danny. "This is no time for games."

Howie yipped and stooped, his front paws straight before him, his tail high in the air. He let them get within a few paces and then ran up the sidewalk.

Danny sighed. But Gilly said, "Come on," and ran after him. C.D. started to run. Ryan shook his head. Danny grabbed him and said, "Come on," in much the same tone that Gilly had used.

It wasn't difficult to keep up with Howie because he always stopped when he got too far ahead. He waited for them, wagging his tail and yipping. Still, Danny hadn't done this much running all at once in a long time. He sweated and breathed hard.

Then Howie zoomed across a park and was lost over a small rise. The kids stood at the edge of the green field waiting for a howl. None came.

"Now what?" Ryan said.

"Follow me," C.D. said. He looked around, and then leaped into the air. As he did, he seemed to close up like a telescope and then flapped away in the form of a bat. The other kids followed as quickly as they could.

C.D. led them across the field of rolling hills to a narrow wooden bridge. A big red dog ran toward them. "Look out!" Ryan cried. It bounded across the bridge and bowled Danny over as it passed. It didn't even slow down. Danny shook his head as Ryan and Gilly helped him to his feet. "I've never seen a dog so scared," Gilly said.

"We must be on the right track," Ryan said.

Across the bridge was a forest that was cool and dim—a swell place for a dog to lose itself. Cheerful water ran along a rocky creek that twisted and crossed among the trees. As they peered into the shadows, hoping for a clue to which way Howie had gone, C.D.—Danny hoped it was C.D.— flapped in circles over their heads and dived into the forest.

In the forest, keeping up with C.D. was difficult. He could fly, but the other kids had to climb over logs and fight through creepers and go around boulders. The first time they came to a creek, Danny looked at how wide it was and how slippery the rocks were and said, "I don't know if I can make it all the way across without slipping into the water."

"Hey, Danny," said Gilly, "you know what the Supremes said: 'Ain't no river wide enough to keep us from Howie.' "

"The Supremes said that?" Ryan said.

"Almost. Give me a minute here." She began to hum one of her mysterious tunes. Gradually a path opened in the water as if somebody had put up a dam. The three kids walked across damp ground to the other side. Gilly stopped singing and the water rushed downstream in a wave. They tramped through the underbrush following C.D.

Danny stopped and looked around. He said, "I lost him."

"Me too," said Ryan.

In a minute C.D, in boy form again, walked between some bushes, taking long drags on his Fluid of Life. When the straw dropped from his mouth he said, "I lost him."

"Well," said Gilly, "that makes it unanimous. Let me try something. Come on." She led them down to another part of the creek. While the boys waited, she got down on her hands and knees and put her ear to the water. She seemed to be listening. She sang a little and listened a little.

She stood up and said, "The water tells me he went that-away."

They ran in the direction Gilly pointed and soon were out of the park and back on a sidewalk. Howie was trotting along about half a block ahead of them. He looked over his shoulder, but did not trot faster. Evidently, he was tired of the game.

Danny should not have been surprised when he found out where Howie was leading them, yet he was. Howie gamboled up to the uniformed doorman of the Talbot Arms. "Hi yah, pooch," the doorman said. "Hi yah."

"Come on, Howie," Danny called. "Dinner." The word "dinner" always got Harryhausen's attention. It got Howie's attention now. But instead of coming over to Danny, he ran to the building's revolving door and sat down. He looked back at the kids and the doorman, obviously waiting for someone to push the door and let him into the building.

The doorman said, "If that's your dog, you better get him out of here. The management don't want any strange dogs around."

Danny had an inspiration. He said, "Howie's not a strange dog. He belongs to the Wolfners."

The doorman rubbed his chin. "Nobody told me about it. And why would they name a dog the same thing as they named their kid?"

Howie barked.

"He sure acts like he lives here. All right," the doorman said and smiled. "But if I find out you kids have been fibbing, that mutt's going to the pound."

"Thanks, mister," Danny, Ryan, and Gilly said. C.D. bowed. They pushed through the revolving door and stood in the lobby waiting for an elevator.

"We have him," Ryan said. "Are we just going to leave him at his house?"

"We couldn't, even if we wanted to," Danny said. "You need a code to get in and I don't know it."

"Then what are we doing in here?" Ryan said.

"Making a plan," Danny said.

"All right," Gilly said, "then let's plan."

"All right," Danny said. "We can't take him to my house. Mom and Dad will want to know who this dog is. And where Howie is. And I'll end up having to tell them that Howie's a werewolf."

"What would they do?" Gilly said.

"Who knows?" said Danny. 'They're parents."

"We must take him to a doctor," C.D. said.

"What kind of doctor?" Ryan said.

That was a good question. "Maybe a psychiatrist," Gilly said. "You know, 'They're coming to take me away, ho ho, ha ha . . .' " She waddled around as if she were drunk and wiggled her finger next to her ear.

"I don't know any psychiatrists," Ryan said.

"I don't either," said Danny, "but I do know a doctor. Dr. Birnberg. I've been going to him since before I can remember."

"Sure," Ryan said. "Your mom recommended him to my mom. He's a nice guy. I like him."

"At the moment," said Gilly, "Howie is a wolf."

The elevator arrived and Howie led the kids on board. The doors closed.

Danny said, "He isn't really a wolf. He just looks like one."

"Indeed," C.D. said. "Inside, he is still a boy."

"Will Dr. Birnberg know that?" Danny said.

"There is a way to find out," Gilly said.

Danny knew what that way was. They all did. Take Howie to Dr. Birnberg and see what happened.

Ryan said, "But can we trust him with Howie?"

C.D. said, "Is he wise enough to find out what is wrong?"

They arrived at the thirtieth floor and Howie sat in front of the doors, waiting for them to open. "Sorry, Howie," Danny said, "I don't know the code. None of us do."

Howie barked and continued to wait. The elevator descended. Howie looked at them reproachfully.

"We'll take him to Dr. Birnberg, then."

"Sounds like a plan to me," said Gilly.


Dr. Birnberg's office was in the mall surrounding the new Buy 'Em—Trade 'Em—Get the Whole Set Building. The kids couldn't get to the mall by bus or by subway because Howie was with them, and a cab was too expensive. By the time they'd walked there, the sun was hovering near the horizon.

Danny went in first to scout the situation. Dr. Birnberg's waiting room had soft couches and chairs. Potted plants stood in the corners. Jaunty recorded music played softly. A pretty woman was sitting at one corner of a couch trying to read a magazine and hold her baby at the same time.

Danny walked to the frosted glass window and knocked. The window slid open and Dr. Birnberg's nurse, Greta, smiled out at him. "Danny," she said. "We didn't expect to see you for another few months."

"Is the doctor here? It's kind of an emergency."

"What's the matter?" Greta stopped smiling, and Danny could tell that she was really concerned.

"It's my friend, Howie. He has a—well, to tell the truth, we don't know what's wrong with him."

"Where is he?"

"Right outside."

"Well, bring him in. Bring him in."

Still not confident that this would work, Danny went to the outside door, and motioned his friends to enter. Greta was standing at the door to the inner office. When she saw Howie she said, "You'll have to leave the dog outside."

"We can't," Danny said. "He's the one who's sick."

Greta frowned. She took a good look at them. "This isn't some kind of joke, is it?"

"No, ma'am," Ryan said. "This is Howie and we're really worried about him."

"But he's a dog."

"Not exactly," Gilly said.

"Huh?"

C.D. said, "She means that Howie is of unusual stock."

"I'm sorry Howie is sick, but you'll have to take him to a veterinarian, an animal doctor. He'll know what to do."

"You think?" Danny said.

"I know that Dr. Birnberg wouldn't have a clue."

They thanked Greta and left. They found a bench in the mall and sat on it while Howie sniffed around a nearby trash can. Danny said, "We'll have to try Dr. Wilma. We take Harryhausen to her for shots and stuff."

C.D. said, "But Howie is not a wolf. He is a werewolf."

"Maybe it'll be all the same to Dr. Wilma," Ryan said.

Gilly said, "At least at a vet's office, they'll let us see the doctor."

"All right," said Danny. "Come on." As they walked, Danny was grateful that Dr. Wilma's office was close. But maybe that wasn't so odd. Lots of doctors and dentists had their offices in the mall.

From the outside, Dr. Wilma's office looked a lot like Dr. Birnberg's. Inside, however it was very different. In Dr. Wilma's waiting room the furniture was made of tough washable plastic and the floor was some kind of green tile that they could just hose down if they had to. Photographs of dogs and cats and parakeets—all kinds of animals—were taped to the walls.

An old man was sitting with a fat calico cat on his lap. "What a Dinah," the man cooed to his cat. Across from him was a young guy dressed like a truck driver. An enormous German shepherd sat between the young guy's feet, but occasionally it got up and tried to make friends with the cat. The cat wasn't having any. When the dog came too close, the cat climbed the old man like a tree. "Down Baskerville," the young guy said to his dog. "Down." The smell was intense. A lot of animals had been there before Howie and the dog and the cat.

The slim lady behind the counter was dressed almost the same way as the truck driver. She wore jeans and a plaid shirt. Instead of heavy work shoes, she wore running shoes. Around her neck she wore a necklace of tiny silver dogs and cats.

Danny told her who he was and who the patient was. She looked over the counter at Howie and said, "He looks very elegant. What's the poor baby's problem?"

Ryan said, "Nothing. It's just kind of a checkup."

The lady nodded and told them to wait. While the kids waited, more people brought in cats and dogs. One little boy had a cage with a hamster in it. Howie wandered around the office, interested in everything. Danny had never seen a nose move so fast. Then Howie sat down on the floor.

A female voice called for Baskerville, and then for Dinah. In a few minutes, the old man came out smiling, and stroking his cat. The voice called, "Howie."

Howie seemed a little reluctant to enter the office, but Danny grabbed him under the front legs and half carried him in. Dr. Wilma pulled the door shut. She was a big woman with short white hair that was almost the same color as the white lab coat she wore. "What seems to be the matter with Howie?" she said. It had been her voice calling each of the patients.

"A check up," C.D. said.

"Ah," said Dr. Wilma. She lifted Howie onto a large aluminum table. She had strong, gentle hands. Howie barked at her.

"Good lungs," Dr. Wilma said. She listened to Howie's heart and looked into his eyes. She pulled his lips back to check his teeth. When she listened to

Howie's heart, she frowned. Whatever was in his eyes made her shake her head. Howie's teeth caused Dr. Wilma to say, "Um," just like a people doctor.

Dr. Wilma scratched Howie behind the ears and said, "I think he's in pretty good shape."

"You think?" C.D. said.

"Well," said Dr. Wilma. She coughed nervously. "Howie doesn't have quite the characteristics of a dog."

"He's a wolf," said Gilly.

"Or a wolf either. I've never seen anything like Howie before. His heartbeat is normal for a dog. But those eyes look more like human eyes. And he has teeth in the back of his mouth that look human too. Where'd you say you got him?"

"He belongs to a friend," Danny said. "But is he healthy?" It suddenly occurred to Danny that visiting the vet was just as useless as visiting the people doctor. They couldn't ask the questions they wanted to ask: What is Howie's problem, and how do we turn him back into a boy?

"His coat looks good and his eyes are clear," Dr. Wilma said. "He's alert and not having any obvious discomfort. I'd say he's healthy. The mystery is, he's a healthy what?"

"Got me," said Ryan.

Danny told the lady at the desk to send the bill for the checkup to the Wolfners' address. He sure didn't want it coming to his house. He'd pay back the Wolfners somehow. He only hoped that they wouldn't be angry when they found out about Howie's problem.

When Howie and the kids got outside, Gilly said, "I think we've run out of types of doctors."

"Time to do something radical," Ryan said.

"Might I suggest Zelda Bella?" C.D. said.

"Who?" Gilly and Ryan asked together.

Danny said, "Once, Howie wanted to be a real boy instead of a werewolf. We tried all kinds of stuff, but the person who got closest to doing what Howie wanted was Zelda Bella."

"She's the one Howie got the familiaides for?" Ryan asked.

"The same," said C.D.

Gilly said, "She must be a witch or something." She and Ryan laughed.

Danny nodded.

Gilly and Ryan stopped laughing.

# Chapter Five

# A Crooked House

As they walked to the mall's exit, Danny and C.D. explained about Zelda Bella. She used to run a fruit store, but now she was Mother Scary on TV, the same Mother Scary who was going to have a special show that very evening.

"I hope we don't miss it," Gilly said.

Danny pushed open the door and was surprised to see how dark it was outside. A reddish glow burned just the other side of Manhattan, so the sun had not quite set, but it was much later than Danny had thought. The air had a chilly edge. Soon he'd have to call his parents again and tell them he and Howie would be even later.

He would have liked to go home right now. But he knew that would be a mistake. His parents would ask a lot of questions about Howie, and Danny would have to give a lot of answers that, up till now, had been secret. If he went home without Howie, the situation would be even worse. The sooner Howie became a boy, the better. Missing Mother Scary's special show was the least of his problems.

"I never met a real witch before," Ryan said.

Danny said, "You're not going to meet a real one tonight unless we can figure out how to get to Halloween Acres. Zelda Bella lives way out on Long Island."

"I have an idea," Gilly said.

C.D. said, "We have no time to put on a show."

"No," said Gilly. "Listen, we can take a cab. We can borrow the money from my mom."

"Your mom will understand?" C.D. said.

"My family is just as much monsters as yours, C.D. She'll understand."

C.D. bowed and told Gilly she was very wise.

They walked through the landscaped sculpture garden that surrounded the Buy 'Em—Trade 'Em—Get the Whole Set Building. Ryan's father had designed the place, and Ryan told them all about it in some detail. Danny couldn't keep his mind on what Ryan was saying.

They walked out onto the main pier of the Stuyvesant Marina. Lights were on and each of them had a tight halo. The smell of the sea was very strong. At number 42, one light was on in the kitchen of the *Capri,* the Finn houseboat. "Looks like nobody's home," Gilly said.

She let them into the main cabin. Howie found lots of interesting smells to investigate while Gilly read the note she found on the kitchen table. "Mom and the aunts are having dinner with their agent." Gilly's mom and aunts were the three Fabulous Finn Sisters. They were popular singers.

"Do we still have cab fare?" Ryan said.

"Right here," Gilly said, and pulled a thick roll of bills from a big conch shell. When she turned around, she saw that her friends were looking at her accusingly. She said, "It's OK for me to take this. Mom told me it was emergency money. Isn't this an emergency?"

Danny said, "Absolutely, Gilly. Thanks. Uh, can I use your phone?"

When his mother answered, Danny said, "Hi, Mom. It's me."

"Danny. Where are you?"

"I'm at Gilly's house with Gilly and Ryan and C.D. and Howie. We're about to go to Zelda Bella's place."

"Isn't that out on Long Island?"

"Gilly's springing for a cab."

"Well," Mrs. Keegan said, astonished.

"We're going to see if we can't help Zelda Bella with her show tonight."

Mrs. Keegan asked more questions, but she knew Danny and Zelda Bella were friends and that Zelda Bella was an adult. Mrs. Keegan promised to update Ryan's and C.D's parents. The last thing Mrs. Keegan said before she hung up was, "Give my love to Howie."

"Sure, Mom," Danny said, and rolled his eyes.

The cab ride lasted half an hour and used most of the money Gilly had taken from the conch shell. By the time they got to Halloween Acres, it was dark. The night's cold edge had begun to bite.

The kids hurried to Zelda Bella's condo with Howie loping alongside. He obviously thought this was some kind of game. Danny rang the door bell. It bonged far away. They waited. Danny rang the door bell again. This time, after the bong, C.D. said, "Someone said, 'Come in.' "

"I didn't hear anything," Ryan said.

"Vampires have many talents," C.D. said.

Danny tried the door and it swung open. It hadn't even been locked. They entered the condo and stood bunched up at the door. It was warm in the room, but that was the only thing Danny liked about it. Not even Howie would venture any farther.

Familiaides were everywhere, jumping on the furniture, playing catch with Zelda Bella's knickknacks, swinging from lamps and light fixtures. A bunch of them were dancing in the empty fireplace. The room looked as if it were very long. And the furniture at the other end looked as if it had been made for a giant.

The room was full of noise too, but none of it seemed to be coming from the familiaides. There were bumps and thumps and the sound of someone dragging a heavy chain. Someone or something moaned. Something else wailed forlornly. The sounds were all around them.

"This isn't what Zelda Bella's condo looked like last time Howie and I were here," Danny said.

"It doesn't look like anybody's condo," Gilly said. She called out, "Zelda Bella?"

"Here," a voice called from far away.

"Up there," C.D. said. He led them across the

room. Familiaides touched them and pulled at them. Danny cried out when one of them jumped onto his shoulder. It didn't do anything. It just rode along, hanging lightly on to Danny's ear.

They could see now that the furniture wasn't really any bigger at the far end of the room. The walls and ceiling of the room converged there. The kids had to stoop as they climbed a flight of stairs. The stairs turned, went up another flight and dead-ended into a wall. The familiaide leaped from Danny's shoulder and ran into the corner. It ran *through* the corner and was gone.

"We can't go the same way the familiaide went," Danny said.

Ryan knocked on the dead-end wall with his knuckles and listened carefully. The moaning and wailing went on, making Danny nervous. Ryan knocked again, and the wall tilted open on a horizontal pivot across its middle.

"Zelda Bella?" Ryan called.

"This way," Zelda Bella called back. She seemed a little closer. Ryan ducked under the pivot. Howie and the other kids followed. The wall clicked shut behind them. Danny looked at where they were and bit his lip.

Gilly turned and tried to tilt the wall again. It wouldn't open. "I don't like this," she said.

"You do not like this?" said C.D. "What do you think of that?"

Gilly put her back to the wall and said, "Ulp."

They were at the end of a long hallway paneled in wood. The floor was a checkerboard of black and white squares. At the other end of it was a small lighthouse. As the light turned, the lighthouse buzzed about as often as the second hand of a clock ticked.

"Where are all the familiaides?" Gilly said.

"Yeah," said Ryan. "If the familiaides won't come here, how good a place can it be?"

"This way," Zelda Bella called. Her voice seemed to be coming from just beyond the lighthouse.

Danny walked slowly along the hallway. He didn't know what he expected to happen, but thoughts of terrible booby traps filled his mind. The kids got to the lighthouse safely and looked at it. It was no taller than Frankie Stein. It seemed to do nothing but turn and buzz. Howie gave it a thorough sniff but seemed to find nothing that interested him.

"Oh no," Ryan said. He pointed down another hallway. At the end of it was another lighthouse, turning and buzzing. There were five hallways, each with a lighthouse at the end. Somehow, even the hallway they'd just walked along now had a lighthouse at other the end.

"Zelda Bella?" Danny said.

"This way."

They walked along a hallway and soon got to another lighthouse. This one was just like the first one. And once more they had five ways to go, each with a lighthouse turning and buzzing at the end.

"I don't like this," Gilly said. "Let's go back the way we came."

C.D. said, "Which way is that?"

None of them knew.

"Zelda Bella," Danny called.

"No need to shout," Zelda Bella said. She sounded as if she were standing at the far end of a hall. Nobody was there, just a lighthouse.

"Where are you?" Gilly said.

"Difficult to say. Where are you?"

Gilly shook her head, and Ryan said, "Difficult to say."

Zelda Bella said, "I think there's something wrong with the familiaides." C.D. walked along the hall toward the sound of Zelda Bella's voice. The others were right behind him. Danny, for one, did not want to be left alone. Zelda Bella said, "This morning they went a little crazy—jumping around and refusing to do what they were told. About that time the condo began to change as if it were some strange lumpy vegetable."

At the next lighthouse, they could still choose from five hallways, but one of them was empty at the end. No lighthouse. Zelda Bella said, "The moans and groans mean that the house is still changing." C.D. ran to the empty intersection and the kids followed. In the center of it, where a lighthouse normally stood, was a hole in the floor.

"Zelda Bella?" C.D. said.

"Still here. What's the story?"

C.D. said, "Her voice comes from down there." He pointed into the hole.

Gilly said, "If there's no way back, we might as well go forward." She sat on the edge of the hole and said, "There's a slide down here."

"Down where?" Zelda Bella said.

"Down where you are," Danny said.

"Am I down?"

Gilly slid off the edge of the hole and dropped out of sight. Her echoing cry of, "Wheee!" came up to Howie and the three boys. Howie barked.

"Let's go," Danny said. He sat on the edge of the hole and took Howie in his arms. "Geronimo!" he cried, and pushed off.

# Chapter Six

# There Is Always a Reason

Immediately, Danny was slipping a zillion miles an hour down a surface so smooth he barely seemed to be touching it. As the warm wind pushed against his face, he gripped Howie tightly not only because he didn't want Howie to jump away, but because he was frightened.

"Get the stor-y-y-y-y!" came Ryan's voice as he dropped onto the slide.

Far away, in the darkness, Danny could see dimly lit rooms. Most of them were right side up. Others were jumbled sideways, and some were even upside down. He thought he saw C.D. sitting alone on the edge of the hole above—if above and below meant anything in Zelda Bella's condo. And they obviously didn't. The darkness beyond his feet told him nothing.

The slide twisted and threw him and Howie across a smooth wooden floor. But it was not as smooth as the slide, and he slid to a stop. Gilly was sitting against the wall next to a closed door trying to keep familiaides out of her hair. This was evidently Zelda Bella's bedroom. The only furniture in it was the bed.

Danny put Howie down and stood up. He just had time to scamper out of the way when Ryan slid into the room followed by C.D. When C.D. and Ryan had untangled, C.D. straightened his tuxedo and looked around. "I suppose," he said, "it would do no good to ask where we are."

"None whatsoever," said Gilly. "But there is that door."

Ryan was still on the floor. He crawled to the door on his hands and knees and knocked.

"Come in," came a muffled voice.

"Zelda Bella?" Ryan said.

"I think so," said the voice.

Ryan got up and opened the door. "It looks like a room."

"That's it?" said Gilly, surprised. "Is it right side up?"

"As far as I can tell," Ryan said.

They walked into the room. A couple of familiaides were twisting the dials on a TV set that stood in one corner. In front of it was a comfy couch covered in a bright pattern of big flowers. While some familiaides used the couch as a trampoline, others pulled the pattern right off the couch and ate it. Danny was amazed. Standing on the table at each end of the couch were lamps formed in the shape of elephants holding torches aloft with their trunks.

The walls were shelves of books—mostly paperbacks, as far as Danny could tell. Next to the door through which they'd entered was a big wooden wardrobe carved with fancy scrollwork.

When the familiaides saw Howie and the kids, a few of them came over to tug at their clothes.

"This is too normal," Danny said as he pulled a familiaide out of his pocket and dropped it onto the floor.

They turned suddenly at the banging and swearing that came from inside the wardrobe. Before they had a chance to do anything, the doors fell open and Zelda Bella tumbled out. She sat on the floor blinking and working her mouth. Familiaides gathered.

"Zelda Bella!" Danny cried.

"That's Mother Scary?" Gilly said.

Ryan said, "She looks different on TV."

"Not Mother Scary at the moment. I'm just plain old mild-mannered Zelda Bella."

"She wears much makeup on TV," C.D. said. Gilly nodded.

"How did you get in there?" Ryan said.

"I don't know. I was following your voices."

"Figures," Gilly said.

Danny said, "I'm sure Howie is sorry the familiaides didn't work out."

Howie barked.

"Not his fault they sent him defective merchandise." Zelda Bella lifted a familiaide from her knee onto the floor, and with a lot of help and grunting, stood up. "What are you kids doing here?"

"It is Howie," C.D. said.

"What is Howie?"

"This," said Danny, and pointed.

"The dog?"

Zelda Bella sat on the couch while Danny explained their problem to her. A line of familiaides stood next to him copying whatever motions he made. Danny tried not to let them make him crazy.

Danny told Zelda Bella that for no reason they could see, Howie had turned into a wolf that morning and stayed that way. They had taken him to a people doctor and to an animal doctor and no one knew what to do. Zelda Bella's mind seemed to be far away, but when Danny finished speaking, she said, "Not your fault, kiddo. Not anybody's fault, except maybe the people who packed those familiaides. Howie has the mongrels."

"The what?" all the kids said together. Howie sat down and paid attention.

"Mongrels. It's a common childhood disease like mumps or chicken pox, but only werewolves can get it."

"You say it is the fault of the people who packed the familiaides?" C.D. said.

"It's a theory. The familiaides don't have mongrels, but they may be carriers." She thought for a moment with her head tilted to one side. "You know," she said brightly, "I'll bet that mongrels is *my* problem too. That cauldron we mixed the familiaides up in is pretty old and it's seen a lot of magic; you never get all the old magic out, no matter how good you clean 'em. I'll bet the combination of mongrels and leftover magic is what made the familiaides crazy and drove them to trashing my condo."

Danny said, "That's interesting, but what can we do about Howie?"

"We don't have to do anything. He'll be a wolf for a week or so and then he'll become himself again.

His folks probably already had mongrels. You can't get it twice."

Danny sank onto the other end of the couch, shaking his head. Howie rested his head on Danny's knee. Danny said, "I can't wait a week. I'm already late getting home. I can't go home *with* Howie. My parents will ask all kinds of embarrassing questions and I'll have to answer them, and the secret of the Brooklyn monsters will be out. I can't go home *without* Howie. That would be even worse."

"Can't your parents keep a secret?" Gilly said.

"Normal secrets, maybe. But monster secrets?" Danny shrugged.

"I don't know if my parents could either," Ryan said.

Zelda Bella stood up and said, "Then we'll have to cure him tonight. Now." She shook her finger at the ceiling.

"Is that possible?" Danny said.

"Hey, kid. Magic is magic, you know? Of course it's possible. I'll whip up a batch of my special dog biscuits. The secret ingredient is garlic." She winked at Danny.

"Isn't there another way?" said Danny.

"I don't think so. Why?"

"Howie and C.D. don't like garlic. It makes them nervous and they change into their animal forms."

"Right you are, kid," Zelda Bella said and snapped her fingers. "But the garlic won't bother Howie. He's already in his animal form. I don't know what we're going to do about C.D."

C.D. said, "Howie is my friend. If there is really no other way to cure him, you may proceed."

"No other way," Zelda Bella said, and shook her head.

"I will be fine," C.D. said. He took a big drink of his Fluid of Life and wrapped himself tightly in his cape.

"You're a great guy," Ryan said.

"Nothing fishy about you," Gilly said.

Howie barked and wagged his tail.

C.D. said, "Let us begin at once. I do not wish to wait."

"Sure, sure. There's just one problem," Zelda Bella said.

"Of course," said C.D. and he bowed.

Zelda Bella chuckled, making light of the problem. "With the shape this condo is in, I don't know where the kitchen is. I don't even know how to get out of this room." She looked at her wrist watch. "And if we don't get out soon, not only will Howie remain a dog, but I'll miss my own show."

Danny said, "You're a witch. Why don't you use your powers to get rid of the familiaides?"

"That's a good question," Zelda Bella said. "A very good question." She continued to nod.

"And the answer is?" Ryan said.

Zelda Bella stopped nodding and shrugged. "The answer is that, uh, these familiaides and what they've done to the condo are neither of them what you would call your average, traditional-type witchy problem. I don't know the solution right off the bat."

"Bat?" said C.D.

"Like in baseball," Ryan said and C.D. nodded.

Zelda Bella said, "The solution might be in my

books, but all my books are downstairs in my workshop.''

"I don't know where the kitchen or the basement is," said Gilly, "but *out* is easy." She danced to the door through which she and the others had entered, and with a flourish, she pulled it open. On the other side was a brick wall. Familiaides piled in front of the wall and, like an ocean wave, rolled right through it as if it weren't there.

"I have an idea for finding the kitchen," Danny said. He held Howie's head in his hands and said, "Dinner, Howie. Find dinner." Howie yipped a time or two and set off with his nose to the floor. Familiaides piled themselves up in shoals to slow him down, and a bunch of them rode on his back. But Howie was single-minded. He looked for dinner. After investigating the entire room, he looked at Danny and whimpered. Danny said, "Go ahead, Howie. Dinner."

Howie used his teeth to pull a cushion off the couch. Beneath it was a stairway. Familiaides tried to hide the entrance, but Howie ran down the stairs in the couch. Zelda Bella followed him, and the kids were right behind.

"This is strange," Danny said. "It looks like we're walking downstairs, but I feel like we're walking upstairs."

"It's an illusion," Zelda Bella said.

"Which?" said Ryan. "The walking up or the walking down?"

"I don't know," Zelda Bella said in frustration. "Ask the tall kid. What's his name, Frankie. He knows all that stuff."

At the end (top or bottom?) of the stairs was a long

hallway with a lighthouse at the end. "This is not good," C.D. said.

"Howie knows where he's going," Danny said. "Come on."

Howie led them from one lighthouse to another. At the end of one hallway was a door like one you might see in any house, except that it was set into the floor. Howie barked at it. Zelda Bella braced herself against the floor with one foot, took hold of the doorknob, and pulled. Nothing happened, so she pushed. Nothing happened. She stood back from the door rubbing her chin.

"Are you sure about this, Howie?" Danny said.

Howie ran between Danny and the door, barking. Then he sniffed at the side of the door where the hinges should have been. Ryan approached the door, rubbed his hands together, and got down on his hands and knees. He pushed lightly with one finger on the side across from the doorknob. The door clicked and swung open. Beyond, Danny could see Zelda Bella's kitchen. But they weren't looking down at it from the ceiling. They were looking across it from one wall. Howie leaped through the doorway.

When it was Danny's turn to leap through, his stomach gave kind of a half twist and he found himself sitting on the floor of the kitchen looking through a regular doorway at the ceiling of the hallway. The kitchen windows were dark, but it was a natural dark. Through them, Danny could see bushes and trees and streetlights.

Familiaides were everywhere in the kitchen, thick as polka dots. They'd pulled things from the cupboards and were playing games with them. Zelda

Bella hustled across the kitchen to a cupboard and said, "Look. They've eaten all the herbs, including the garlic."

Familiaides were sitting in the spice cabinet shoveling dry green leaves into each other's mouths. One of the familiaides was taking big bites out of the spice cabinet itself.

"I guess you're all out of garlic," Ryan said.

"Oh, that's not a problem," Zelda Bella said. "I have a plot of it growing in the backyard." She opened the kitchen door and stopped. The kids looked around her.

Outside the door was the living room. They were standing in the fireplace, none of them any bigger than a familiaide. A couple of familiaides ran toward them, but Zelda Bella slammed the door before they got there.

"Very spooky," Gilly said.

"Yeah, well," Zelda Bella said and shrugged. But she looked disheartened.

Ryan climbed onto the sink and slid up the lower sash of a window.

"Good idea," said Zelda Bella.

Ryan poked his head out the opening, and brought it right back in. "Not such a good idea. Have a look." He moved to one side.

If Danny looked outside through the glass part of the window, he still saw a normal nighttime scene. If he looked out through the opening, he saw Zelda Bella's bedroom.

Zelda Bella said, "Close that window and come on down here. We have to think this through."

Zelda Bella and the kids sat around the kitchen

table while Howie sat under the table among their feet. C.D. sucked on his Fluid of Life. Zelda Bella said, "The first thing we have to do is make my house normal again."

"This does not require garlic?" C.D. said.

"Who knows?" Zelda Bella said.

They pondered Zelda Bella's proposal.

Danny said, "Let's look at the instructions that came with the familiaides. Maybe we'll find a clue."

Zelda Bella rummaged through a kitchen drawer and brought a piece of paper back to the table. She smoothed it out with the flat of her hand and said, "Not much here. It says 'just add water.' "

"Adding water started our troubles," Danny said.

Ryan took the paper from Zelda Bella and read it through. "It says, 'If not completely satisfied, return unused familiaides to England.' "

"Great," said Gilly sarcastically.

Ryan said, "If we can't solve the condo problem, maybe we should try to solve Howie's problem."

"Is good," C.D. said. He pounded on the table and they all jumped. "I have an idea."

Zelda Bella said, "Spit it out, boy. I'm all ears."

"Spit?" said C.D. "Ears?"

"What's your idea?" Danny said.

"Ah," said C.D. "Is it not correct that the familiaides were made to help?"

"Originally," Danny said.

C.D. nodded and said, "Then let us ask them to help."

Zelda Bella pursed her lips as if she were whistling. No sound came out. She said, "It couldn't hurt." She stood up and pointed at a group of familiaides who were in the corner playing catch with raisins. "All right, men. Enough of this lollygagging. Time for work. Get out to my garden and bring me a bouquet of garlic. Just pull up the green weedy things that look like green onions. The white garlic cloves are underground. Hop to it."

The familiaides scrambled to the corner and hopped through the bend where the two walls met.

"Well, what do you know about that?" Zelda Bella said. "They did what I told 'em."

Danny was as surprised as anybody else, but they didn't have time to discuss the familiaides' sudden cooperation. The condo began to shake.

"Earthquake!" Ryan cried.

# Chapter Seven

# The Case of the Crazy Quilt Condo

Ryan dived under the table, and the others crouched down there with him. The condo squeaked and moaned. Great crashing sounds echoed. The walls of the kitchen seemed to fold open and close in at the same time. Beyond them Danny saw vast black reaches of star-flung space. He felt as if he were being turned inside out and then turned outside out. He closed his eyes and mentally tried to get ahold of himself.

It was pretty crowded under the table, but the earthquake didn't last long. Loose things stopped shaking, the joints of the condo stopped squeaking. When it was over, everybody just sat there under the kitchen table breathing hard.

"What was that?" said Gilly.

"Not your average earthquake," Danny said and described what had happened to him. They each had had a similiar experience.

They crawled from under the table and stood up, looking around. "The kitchen looks the same to me," Gilly said.

Ryan said, "As a reporter, I suggest we investigate."

"Indeed," C.D. said and began to look around. Danny opened cupboards and looked into the oven. Gilly turned the water taps on and off. Ryan and C.D. made minute inspections of the furniture.

"Sheesh," said Gilly, "the water in the tap tells a strange story. Evidently, it wasn't just the rooms in the condo that got mixed up. The water has been in places water was not meant to go."

"What places?" Danny said.

"Can I get some help over here?" Zelda Bella said.

"You'd rather not know, trust me," said Gilly, and the kids went to help Zelda Bella.

She said, "The door to the dining room slammed shut. Now it's stuck." She pulled on it, but it wouldn't open.

"Perhaps this," C.D. said as he turned a key-shaped handle. Something in the door clicked and it swung open.

"Well now, look at this," said Zelda Bella.

The last time Danny had looked through this doorway, he'd seen the ceiling of the lighthouse hallway. Now, he saw Zelda Bella's dining room. It was right side up and otherwise absolutely normal. There weren't even any familiaides in it. That is what should have been there, but somehow Danny hadn't expected it.

The familiaides in the kitchen ignored the open doorway. Howie, however, sniffed at the border between the kitchen and the dining room, then trotted through the doorway. He sat on the floor and scratched himself.

"It's really there," Zelda Bella said.

"This is weird," Gilly said.

"Yeah," said Ryan. "Normal is weird."

"Normal is weird?" Danny said. "That's weird."

"But what does it mean?" C.D. said. "Perhaps the garlic is no longer necessary?"

"I wouldn't go that far," Zelda Bella said. "But the return of my dining room ought to tell us something about how the familiaides confused my condo."

"Let's think about this," Ryan said. "The familiaides confused your condo. Then some of the familiaides left to get garlic from your garden. The earthquake, or whatever it was, happened right after the familiaides left."

"Yeah," said Gilly. "And *how* did they leave?"

"That's a different question. My readers and I want to know if there's any connection between the familiaides leaving and the earthquake."

"Your readers?" Danny said.

"Sure. 'The Case of the Crazy Quilt Condo.' It'll make a great story in the school paper."

Danny said, "You'll have to leave out the part about Howie being a werewolf."

"Of course."

"And the part about Zelda Bella being a real witch."

"Sure." Ryan considered what Danny had just said. He shook his head and said, "Maybe I should just take up writing science fiction."

"Ryan asks a good question," C.D. said. "Is there a connection between the exiting familiaides and the earthquake?"

"Maybe there is," Zelda Bella said. She walked around tapping her front teeth with a finger. She turned on the kids suddenly and said, "Suppose the condo isn't stable the way it is. Suppose it's like a house of cards. The only thing keeping it up in its confused form is the presence of the familiaides.''

"Go on," C.D. said.

"OK. Then suppose when they went outside for the garlic, the house collapsed a little into its normal form because they weren't here to hold it up."

"I wish Frankie were here," Danny said, "but it sounds good to me. To make the condo entirely normal, all we have to do is send the familiaides back where they came from."

"Where's that?" said Gilly. "England?"

"Farther away than that," said Zelda Bella.

"Mars?" Danny said. "The fourth dimension?"

"New Jersey?" Ryan said.

"Maybe not that far," Zelda Bella said. "My guess is that they'll be folded into the very fabric of the condo. Like nuts into cookie batter."

"This means what?" said C.D.

"It means," said Zelda Bella, "they'll be safely out of the way. They won't be hurt and they won't be able to hurt anybody. They'll just be gone. Get it?"

"Got it," said C.D. sounding only a little bewildered.

There was a knock at the kitchen door.

As Zelda Bella ran to answer it she said, "I hope that's somebody from the outside world." She opened the door. Most of the doorway was black, but at the bottom was a fireplace-size hole. All that black is the inside of the chimney, Danny thought. As the familiaides marched from the fireplace into the kitchen Ryan said, "At least the fireplace is the right size again."

Each familiaide was carrying something. A few of them carried a tree branch between them like a stretcher.

One had a flower. Three others carried an old bird cage over their heads. As they walked, they left little sooty footprints. Not one of them carried garlic or anything remotely like it. They dropped this stuff before Zelda Bella, bowed deeply, and ran to mix among their friends.

"No garlic," said C.D., sounding relieved.

"They must have come down the chimney," Danny said. "I guess they can't come through walls when they're carrying something."

Ryan said, "Now we know why they were so cooperative."

"Yeah," said Gilly. "It was another gag. They just wanted to give us false hope."

"And do more mischief," C.D. said.

"Go away!" Zelda Bella cried, gesturing at the familiaides. "Go away!" When the familiaides ignored her, Zelda Bella smiled with resignation and said, "I had to try just to make sure."

"Let me try something else," Gilly said. She stepped forward and began to sing. It was a scary song that certainly made Danny want to go back where he'd come from. Instead of sending them away, the song attracted the familiaides. They stood around whistling and applauding and stamping their feet.

Danny and Ryan made faces at the familiaide crowd. The familiaides only pointed and laughed.

"This isn't working," said Zelda Bella. She sounded hysterical.

"I have an idea," C.D. said. He knelt before Howie and said, "Howie, you must howl for us. You must howl your most frightening."

Howie had been sitting on the floor with his head

**66**

in his paws, but he seemed to understand C.D. He scratched himself, stood up, threw his head back, and howled. It was a terrible noise from the dawn of time, from before people had pets, from some savage age when a frightening voice was sometimes all that kept away your enemies. Danny had to hang on to the furniture or his hands would shake.

At the first note of Howie's howl, the familiaides turned to look at him. They began to dance around as if on a hot griddle, and then they jumped out of the kitchen through the cracks in the walls. As familiaides poured out of the room, another earthquake began, this one stronger than the other.

Once again Zelda Bella and Howie and the kids dived under the kitchen table. The room shook as Howie continued to howl. Walls folded through strange angles. Windows blinked as if the sun had hurriedly come up and then dropped out of the sky. The floor and ceiling traded places again and again, then they began to close in. Danny watched in horror as the kitchen shrank. If it didn't stop soon, they would all be crushed!

# Chapter Eight

# Catching Flies With Their Tongues

With a terrific crash the kitchen door popped open and banged against a counter. Danny grabbed Howie and crawled across the kitchen floor, hoping it wouldn't become a ceiling all of a sudden. The kitchen was not much bigger than a bathroom and getting smaller all the time.

"Come on," Danny cried, but didn't have time to look back and see if his friends were following. At the moment the doorway was just big enough for a dog about Howie's size, but it was shrinking too. Danny pushed Howie through and once again cried, "Come on." A bat flashed past him. Danny clambered after Howie and suddenly everything was dark and quiet.

Danny didn't move. Somewhere banging and crashing continued, but it may as well have been in another universe. Much closer, Danny heard normal night sounds. He heard crickets and the drone of traffic. Far away, someone laughed and stopped abruptly. The air was cool but not unpleasant and it smelled of night-blooming flowers.

Then Danny noticed little points were poking him all over. As near as he could tell, he was in a bush outside the front window of the condo. "Wow," he said. "Are you guys OK?" He jumped onto the lawn and looked around as he pulled leaves and twigs from his hair and clothes. He was alone. He was alone, but at least he was outside.

The banging and crashing continued. It seemed to be coming from inside the condo, though from here, the condo looked normal. Lights were on in every room, but as far as he could tell, each room was where it belonged and right side up. He could not see a lighthouse or a familiaide.

"Howie?" Danny called. He was worried that the earthquake had frightened Howie so much that he'd run away again. And where was everybody else?

"Howie? Gilly?" Danny called. "Ryan? C.D.? Zelda Bella?" He walked around the side of the condo and found Ryan unwinding Gilly from a garden hose. "Where's C.D. and Zelda Bella?" Danny asked. "And have you seen Howie?"

"Howie's missing?" Gilly said, astonished.

"It looks like it," Danny said. "I'll never be able to go home."

"You know what Howie would say," Ryan said. "He'd say, 'Stiff upper lip, Keegan. Stiff upper lip.' "

"Yeah. That's what he'd say, all right." Danny tried to feel better, but it was an uphill push. He ran around to the back and found Zelda Bella sitting on the steps fluffing her hair. "Pretty exciting, huh?" Zelda Bella said.

"That's for sure. Where's C.D. and Howie?"

"I don't know. Howie went through with you, didn't he?"

"Just ahead of me," Danny said. "Maybe it made a difference. We all went through the same door and came out in different places."

"He'll be back," Zelda Bella said. "Come on and help me find some garlic."

"What about C.D.?" Danny looked into the dark sky and thought he saw something even darker flapping around.

"He's around here someplace. Come on."

It was dark in the garden, and Zelda Bella kept showing Danny things he couldn't see. "Here's rutabaga. And it looks as if the wolfsbane is coming up real nice."

While she was walking down the rows looking for the garlic, an old guy wearing a baseball cap and a couple of women in jogging clothes wandered up. The guy said, "You OK, Zelda Bella?"

"Just fine, Jack." Zelda Bella stood up. "How are you and Sarah?"

"We're all right," Sarah said. "But I've never heard such noise as is coming out of your condo."

They listened to more booming. Then something tinkled and sprang and boomed all at once; it sounded as if a grandfather clock had fallen over. Zelda Bella said, "Just doing a little remodeling. Nothing to worry about."

C.D. walked out of a shadow and snapped his cape open.

Staring at C.D., Jack said, "As long as you're fine." He and the others hurried off.

"Have you seen Howie?" Danny said.

"He is missing?" C.D. said and looked around worriedly.

"Ah," Zelda Bella said. "Here it is."

Gilly and Ryan walked up. They all watched as Zelda Bella bent over to grab a green stalk at its base. Zelda Bella looked over her shoulder and said, "You'd better go, C.D. When I pull this garlic out of the ground, it'll start to smell."

C.D. bowed and leaped into the air as a bat. As he flapped away, Danny called after him, "And look for Howie while you're up there!"

Zelda Bella pulled the stalk from the ground and straightened up as she brushed dirt from the white bulb at its nether end. "Garlic," she said and smacked her lips. "Food o' the gods. Too bad your friends have such trouble with it."

As they walked back to the kitchen they kept a lookout for Howie, but they didn't see him. When they got to the kitchen door, Zelda Bella peered in at the window. The crashing and banging had stopped.

"Looks good to me," she said.

"We were fooled by windows before," Ryan said.

"No matter what," Gilly said, "we can't stand out here all night."

Zelda Bella grabbed the doorknob and twisted it. She winked at the kids, and with a single yank she pulled the door open.

"Looks like a kitchen to me," Danny said.

"The proof is in the entering," Zelda Bella said. She strode forward and soon stood in the center of the room nodding. "Looks OK to me," she said. "Come on in and shut the door."

She set the garlic on the table and said, "I need a cookbook."

"You have cookbooks here," Danny said, and pointed.

"The one I have in mind is kind of special. I'll show you." She led them through the house—all normal—and to a closet where she pulled open a trapdoor that filled most of the closet's floor.

Zelda Bella flicked on a light, and they went down a stairway into a room that seemed to take up all the space under the condo. The room was dim, and everything in it cast long shadows in the light of bare electric bulbs. Thick ceramic bowls, glass tubes, and brass measuring devices were lined up on long tables. Against the walls were thick heavy bookcases that held enormous leather-bound volumes. Some of the volumes looked very old and weathered. None of them looked new. Danny laid his hand on a table and pulled it away suddenly when he saw what he'd almost put his hand on: a candle attached by its own drips to a skull.

"Wow," said Ryan, "a real witch's laboratory."

"You better believe it, sweetie. Don't touch anything or you could end up catching flies with your tongue." She chuckled. Or could it have been a cackle?

"Yuck," said Ryan.

The kids gathered in the center of the room and stood there as if tied together.

Zelda Bella said, "Oh, for gosh sakes, you can look around. Just don't touch anything." She turned to peruse her tomes and said, "Now, let me see."

Nests of cobwebs were in all the corners, and once Danny saw a big black spider walk across the room, moving as if it were controlled by clockwork. In the spaces between bookcases were astrological charts, pictures of the human body, and racks full of glassware in strange shapes.

"Here it is," said Zelda Bella and pulled down a book almost as big as a TV tray.

"That's a cookbook?" said Gilly.

"There's all kinds of cooking," said Zelda Bella confidentially.

She clutched the book against her chest, and everybody went back upstairs. In the kitchen, Zelda Bella laid the book on the table and opened it. The pages were made of some thick yellowish paper, and the words, though written in recognizable letters, were not in English.

"Is that Latin?" said Ryan.

"It's Witch," said Zelda Bella.

They all nodded and said "ah" as if they understood. Danny wondered how much of what Zelda Bella told them was true, and how much of it was, as Gilly would say, show biz.

Zelda Bella turned page after page, mumbling to herself. At last she said, "It says here the garlic needs to be dried, not fresh." She held up the garlic like a bell.

"How dry I am," said Gilly and began to sing.

"What?" said Zelda Bella as the garlic began to hiss and shrivel. Steam rose from the garlic to form a cloud against the ceiling. As the cloud rolled and grew, there was a tiny clap of thunder, and forks of lightning no bigger than real forks flashed. Zelda Bella slammed her cook tome shut and leaned over it to protect it from the misty rain that fell.

"Oops, sorry," Gilly said. She sang another song, and soon the clouds broke up and rolled out a window.

While Danny and Ryan mopped the floor, Gilly helped Zelda Bella wipe down the table. When everything was dry, Zelda Bella opened her tome again. She said, "All right," and brushed her hair back with the back of one hand. "Get me a big bowl and some flour."

That was just the beginning. She kept the kids hopping, and after a while they had most of the contents of the cupboards out on the kitchen table.

As she mixed and measured, Zelda Bella spoke spells. Some of them had to be sung. "Hey, that's pretty catchy," Gilly said, and she tried to sing harmony. Zelda Bella smiled and nodded and sang louder as she poured and stirred.

Pretty soon, she was conducting with her big wooden spoon and singing "That Old Black Magic" with Gilly.

Danny and Ryan watched in amazement. Danny could not help thinking that all this would go for nothing if they couldn't find Howie.

# Chapter Nine

# The Old Double Shuffle

The singing and dancing were over. The garlic dog biscuits were in the oven, and the condo was filling with wonderful smells that would have driven any werewolf or vampire crazy. Zelda Bella and the kids sat around her kitchen table drinking big glasses of tap water. Conversation was sparse and distracted. They were all thinking about Howie and the fact that he wasn't back yet.

After fifteen minutes of this, Zelda Bella pulled the sheet of dog biscuits from the oven and set it on the sink to cool.

"I guess Howie'll show up pretty soon," Danny said in as light a tone as he could manage.

"He'd better," Zelda Bella said as she looked at the kitchen clock. "I have to leave in a few minutes." She laughed nervously. "Can't have a Mother Scary show without Mother Scary."

Something scratched at the door. Their eyes widened and Danny tried not to hope too much. It could be just a cat. There were plenty of them around.

Zelda Bella opened the door, and Howie trotted into the kitchen looking very proud of himself. He carried a familiaide that struggled in his mouth. Wagging his tail, Howie set the familiaide down in front of Danny. When the familiaide was loose, it scampered for the wall, but instead of going through, it bounced off. This surprised it. It shook its head, found the bend where two walls met, and this time managed to escape. Howie barked twice.

"Thank Howie for the nice present," Zelda Bella said.

"Thanks, Howie." Danny looked at Zelda Bella and said, "I think he deserves a reward, don't you? A nice dog biscuit."

Howie barked and stood on his hind legs.

"Sounds like a yes vote to me," Zelda Bella said. She lifted the biscuits from the sheet with a metal spatula. Danny took one. It was warm but not hot, and it smelled delicately of garlic. "Here, Howie," Danny said, and dropped the biscuit into Howie's mouth. He swallowed it almost without chewing and barked, demanding another one.

Howie ate three more dog biscuits before he had enough. He sniffed at the fourth one, but didn't eat it.

"He looks like he's smiling," Ryan said.

"That's a start," Danny said.

"Well," said Zelda Bella, "we've done all we can. The rest is up to Howie. And I'm going to be late if I don't get on my Broom right now."

"Broom?" Ryan said.

"You'll see," Zelda Bella said. "I have just time to drop you kids at somebody's house if we get moving right now."

Zelda Bella collected her great fringed purse, Cthulhu, threw on a long denim coat, and in moments was out the door. The kids collected outside her garage and waited. A mechanical rumbling began inside, and a second later Zelda Bella backed up a big black car that had the shape and shine of a beetle. It was a beautiful aerodynamic thing.

Danny, Gilly, and Ryan piled into the backseat with Howie on the floor. There was plenty of room. The inside of this old car was bigger than the inside of some modern vans. They buckled up.

"I thought you said you had a broom," Gilly said as Zelda Bella backed down the driveway like a fiend.

"This is it," Zelda Bella said. "My 1956 Broom. It's a very popular make in Rumania."

Danny and Ryan glanced at each other. They didn't quite believe Zelda Bella, though it was possible what she said was true.

At the end of the driveway, Zelda Bella said, "Where are we going, anyway?"

"My house," said Danny. "Howie's parents are probably there by now."

Gilly and Ryan said it was fine by them.

Danny gave Zelda Bella directions to his house. The car slid into the street and the engine hummed with massive power. The ride was so smooth, Danny felt as if he were traveling in a spaceship. As the Broom roared down the street a small black figure flapped just above the big broomlike hood ornament.

"C.D." Ryan cried.

"I knew he wouldn't go far," Danny said. "He would want to make sure Howie was OK."

With C.D. their constant companion, the Broom boomed through the night, back into the more settled and civilized parts of Long Island. Howie yawned and curled up on the floor to sleep.

"That's a good sign," Danny said. He felt better now. If only he could be sure Howie would change before they got to his house.

At stoplights, C.D. rested on the hood ornament, gripping it with his claws like a bird. Streetlights swept through the windows of the car, now and again illuminating Howie as he rocked gently with the car. Danny watched him, waiting for the change to begin.

Traffic was not heavy, and it didn't take long for them to get to Brooklyn. As they rolled through a more familiar part of town, Danny watched Howie with fascination. His ears shortened, his nose became more of a pug, and his hair receded.

"It's working," Danny said excitedly.

"What did you expect?" Zelda Bella said.

Danny shrugged and laughed. "Yeah, sure." He was so relieved that he could go home that he would have believed almost anything Zelda Bella told him.

"This is getting to be embarrassing," Gilly said. She looked out the window to avoid looking at Howie.

"Yeah," said Danny. "I hadn't thought of that."

"Can we borrow your coat, Zelda Bella?" Ryan said.

"Gosh. You're right. I hadn't thought about clothes either. Sure. Take the coat."

Danny pulled the coat off the front seat, and with Ryan's help, got it onto Howie. It fit him like a tent, but at least he was covered, and he wouldn't freeze.

"You can look now, Gilly," Danny said.

Howie's paws grew fingers and flattened into hands. By the time they got to Danny's neighborhood, Howie was a boy again. Danny sighed.

As they turned onto Danny's block, he prodded Howie with a toe and said, "Howie, we're almost there. You have to wake up."

"Hm?" said Howie. He blinked and sat up. "Where are we?"

Ryan said, "In Zelda Bella's Broom."

"What?" He looked around. "I've had a most interesting dream."

"I'm a 'Daydream Believer,' " Gilly said.

Danny said, "You had the mongrels."

"Really?" Howie sounded fascinated. "You'll have to tell me about it, old chum. I don't remember much."

"Later," said Danny. "We're here."

Zelda Bella pulled the Broom into the Keegan driveway and the kids piled out. Danny stuck his head back into the car and said, "Thanks for everything, Zelda Bella. We'll get your coat back to you soon. And have a good show."

"Don't say that," said Gilly. "It's bad luck. Break a leg, Zelda Bella!"

"Thank you for thanking me. Gotta fly."

Danny slammed the car door. The Broom backed out of the driveway, and with a screech of tires, took off down the street.

"Hope she makes it," Gilly said.

C.D. landed near them and turned into a boy. He took a hard pull from his Fluid of Life and bowed to Howie. Howie bowed back. He looked a little strange wearing Zelda Bella's coat. It came down to his knees. He shuffled from bare foot to bare foot. The ground must have been plenty cold.

"You are fine, I see," C.D. said.

"Fine fettle," Howie said, smiling. He and C.D. shook hands.

As they walked to the front door, Howie said, "That's my parents' car," and pointed to an old station wagon parked at the curb. It was the kind that had real wooden sides. "Is it still Friday?" Howie said.

"You better believe it," Danny said, and laughed.

"Tough time, eh, old man?" Howie said.

"You have no idea," Danny said. He used his key to open the front door. "We're home," he called. "Ryan and C.D. and Gilly are with us."

"Come in, come in," Mrs. Keegan called.

Mr. Keegan said, "We were just beginning to wonder where you kids—" The kids entered the dining room where the Keegans were serving tea to the Wolfners. Barbara was there too, eating fancy company cookies and drinking milk. In the center of the table was Barbara's ice-cream-stick fort, now completed. It looked so good to Danny, he wondered how much of it their father had made.

Mrs. Wolfner was a handsome woman with long silver hair. Mr. Wolfner was a short wide man whose red hair was thinning a little on top. At the moment, they and the Keegans were staring at Howie. Mrs. Wolfner said, "Howie! What happened to your clothes?"

"Actually, mum, there was a small accident."

"Accident?" Mr. Wolfner said.

"Nothing serious, I assure you. Only somewhere

along the line, I seem to have lost my clothes. Zelda Bella was kind enough to lend me her coat."

"Sounds like quite a story," Mr. Keegan said.

"Yeah," said Barbara.

Everybody waited to hear the story.

Mrs. Wolfner glanced at her husband and stood up. She said, "Right-o then. The important thing is that Howie is safe now." She extended a hand to Mrs. Keegan and said, "Thank you so much for the tea. But it's been a long trip in from Mt. Palomine Observatory, and Lon and I are eager to get home. You understand, I'm sure. Howie, thank the Keegans for their hospitality this week and get ready to go."

Danny knew that the Wolfners didn't want Howie to explain the "accident" if it had anything to do with their being werewolves. The Wolfners were giving his parents the old double shuffle, and he could see by the expression on their faces that they knew it too. Mr. Keegan said, "No problem. We enjoyed having him. But we're a little concerned about the accident. Ouch." Mrs. Keegan had kicked her husband to stop him from being too inquisitive.

Barbara grumbled, "Danny has all the good adventures."

Nobody moved. Something had to be done quickly or Howie would be forced by politeness to tell about the mongrels. They needed a diversion. Danny said, "Hey, look. It's eight o'clock! Time for the special Mother Scary show."

Barbara leaped to her feet and said, "Can I watch it, Mom? Can I? Can I?" Good old Barbara, Danny thought. She'd done exactly what he knew she'd do.

Gilly said, "I'd like to watch too, Mr. and Mrs.

Keegan. I designed the special machine Mother Scary's going to use.''

"Jolly good," Howie said.

"I suppose so," Mrs. Keegan said, looking as if things were moving a little fast for her.

As everybody went into the living room, Barbara sidled up to Danny and whispered, "If you don't tell me all about your adventure, I'll make up something really awful to tell Mom and Dad.''

"They'd never believe you," Danny whispered back.

"They might believe some of it," Barbara whispered.

"Later," said Danny. He ran to the TV and turned it on. After finding the right channel, he and the others sat through a Wonky Wheats commercial. When it was over, Mother Scary's theme music began. It played through twice, which was unusual enough, and then the TV showed her bubbling cauldron. A long time seemed to go by before Mother Scary hurried into the scene and skidded to a stop.

"I guess her timing was pretty close," Ryan said.

Innocently, Mr. Keegan said, "That Zelda Bella is a wonderful woman, lending Howie her coat and all." He waited again for some details of the adventure, but Howie only politely agreed with him. Barbara smirked. Danny wondered if he could trust her with the truth. She already knew his friends were monsters and as far as he knew, she'd never told anybody. He'd let Howie decide.

"She does not look entirely like herself," C.D. said.

"Her hat's on crooked," Ryan said. "That's for sure.''

Gilly nodded. "And her makeup looks a little

sketchy. She must have made it to the studio by seconds.''

Mr. and Mrs. Keegan nodded. No further pearls fell from Gilly's lips.

"Tonight," Mother Scary said, "I have a new kitchen helper for all you ghosts, ghouls, and gobblins out there. It's an infernal machine that's the wonder of the age. I give you the *Vegetizer*."

She pulled a table up next to her cauldron. On it was a small guillotine with two holes. A carrot had been shoved through the lower one. The blade was up and ready. "It slices. It dices. And unlike other sharp objects in the kitchen, the Vegetizer will never cut you.''

As she spoke, she put her finger through the top hole. Danny hoped she knew what she was doing. Suddenly, she thrust the blade home. It made a terrible crunching noise and the front part of the carrot fell onto the table.

Mother Scary made a horrified face and for a moment, Danny was sure she'd cut off her finger. Then she cackled and pulled her finger from the guillotine and waved it in front of the camera. It was still connected to her hand. "The Vegetizer," she cried. "Today's infernal machine for today's kitchen!" She cackled again.

Barbara shook her head. "Pretty lame," she said.

Gilly said, "That's a very old trick. Do you want to know how it's done?''

"I am not certain," C.D. said. He sucked on his Fluid of Life.

Mother Scary threw the Vegetizer over her shoulder and said, "Speaking of infernal machines, tonight's special movie is the Max Googleman classic, *The Infernal Machine*. It's the old black and white version. Nobody's taken the trouble to colorize *this* baby." She cackled. "Not only that, but we're going to show *The Infernal Machine* on an infernal machine! I give you now an infernal machine designed by Gilly Finn, built and played by Elisa and Frankie Stein!"

Mother Scary got a surprised look on her face. At first Danny thought it was part of the show, but then something under Mother Scary's clothes began to move around. She looked down her front, and cried, "Eek! Commercial! Cut to a commercial!"

A small black thing leaped from Mother Scary's neckline and ran across the floor. The camera followed it across cables and chalk marks. Cameramen tried to pull their cameras out of its way.

Howie said, "Why, it's a familiaide!"

"What's a familiaide?" Mr. Keegan said.

Before anybody had a chance to give even an evasive answer, the familiaide scurried past Frankie, who was holding the two handles of a big bellows that made up one end of a strange looking machine, what looked to Danny like a hurdy-gurdy from Mars. As the familiaide climbed knobs and levers to the top of the infernal machine, the camera pulled back, and they could see Elisa at its other end, sitting at a thing like the keyboard of a piano. Both Frankie and Elisa looked astonished.

"Go ahead," Mother Scary whispered to them. But the whisper was amplified so everybody could hear it.

Still staring at the familiaide, Frankie began to

pump the bellows and Elisa started to play the keyboard. The infernal machine began to play Mother Scary's theme song, but it was accompanied by blasts of laser light, puffs of smoke, and turning mirrored balls. Fireworks exploded from the back of the machine. Static and wavy lines played across a TV screen on the front of it.

When the music started, the familiaide began to dance, which seemed to go just right with the rest of the performance. The movie *The Infernal Machine* began to roll on the little screen. The camera came in for a close-up.

"There's no business like show business, is there?" said Gilly.

"Jolly good entertainment, all riqht," Howie said. "I am delighted I didn't miss it."

"Me too," said Danny. He was glad Howie was back in his kid form, of course. But not just because he didn't want Howie to miss the show. Danny was glad to be able to come home. Even without Mother Scary's special show, that would have been a very good thing indeed.

MEL GILDEN is the author of the acclaimed *The Return of Captain Conquer*, published by Houghton Mifflin in 1986, and *Harry Newberry and the Raiders of the Red Drink*, published by Henry Holt and Company. Prior to these novels, Gilden had short stories published in such places as *Twilight Zone— The Magazine*, *The Magazine of Fantasy and Science Fiction*, and many original and reprint anthologies. He is also the author of ten previous hair-raising Avon Camelot adventures featuring Danny Keegan and his fifth grade monster friends, *M Is For Monster*, *Born To Howl*, *The Pet Of Frankenstein*, *Z Is For Zombie*, *Monster Mashers*, *Things That Go Bark In The Park*, *Yuckers!*, *The Monster In Creeps Head Bay*, *How To Be A Vampire In One Easy Lesson*, and *Island Of The Weird*.

JOHN PIERARD is a freelance illustrator living in Manhattan. He is best known for his science fiction illustrations for *Isaac Asimov's Science Fiction Magazine*, *Distant Stars*, and SPI games such as *Universe*. He is co-illustrator of Time Machine #4: *Sail With Pirates* and Time Traveler #3: *The First Settlers*, and is illustrator of Time Machine #11: *Mission to World War II*, Time Machine #15: *Flame of the Inquisition*, and the "Fifth Grade Monsters" series: *M Is For Monster*, *Born To Howl*, *The Pet Of Frankenstein*, *There's A Batwing In My Lunchbox*, *Z Is For Zombie*, *Monster Mashers*, *Things That Go Bark In The Park*, *Yuckers!*, *The Monster In Creeps Head Bay*, *How To Be A Vampire In One Easy Lesson*, and *Island Of The Weird*.

# HOWLING GOOD FUN
# FROM AVON CAMELOT

**WEREWOLF, COME HOME**      75908-X/$2.75 US/$3.25 CAN

**HOW TO BE A VAMPIRE IN ONE EASY LESSON**
                             75906-3/$2.75 US/$3.25 CAN

**ISLAND OF THE WEIRD**      75907-1/$2.75 US/$3.25 CAN

**THE MONSTER IN CREEPS HEAD BAY**
                             75905-5/$2.75 US/$3.25 CAN

**THINGS THAT GO BARK IN THE PARK**
                             75786-9/$2.75 US/$3.25 CAN

**YUCKERS!**                 75787-7/$2.75 US/$3.25 CAN

**M IS FOR MONSTER**         75423-1/$2.75 US/$3.25 CAN

**BORN TO HOWL**             75425-8/$2.50 US/$3.25 CAN

**THERE'S A BATWING IN MY LUNCHBOX**
                             75426-6/$2.75 US/$3.25 CAN

**THE PET OF FRANKENSTEIN**  75185-3/$3.50 US/$3.25 CAN

**Z IS FOR ZOMBIE**          75686-2/$2.75 US/$3.25 CAN

**MONSTER MASHERS**          75785-0/$2.75 US/$3.25 CAN